THE ALIEN'S SUFFERING

GRACE KENSINGTON

1

Kyven tossed another piece of dried brush onto the fire that they had built and sat back on his heels to stare into the glow of the flames. The light breeze that was blowing through the camp that they had set up was making the fire dance and spark, and he felt himself worry that someone was going to see the glow or the smoke and come after them. Even as the thought moved through his mind, however, he wondered who it would be that would have the most reason for pursuing them, and what would happen even if they did.

He knew from what Athan had told them that they were all now on the bad side of the Order, putting themselves at serious risk by stealing the vehicles and embarking on this journey to find out more about his father. The thought scared him. He didn't remember as much about the Order from his childhood that Maxim did, but what he did remember let him know that they would not take the betrayal of one of their own or the unauthorized use of technology that had been made out of bounds lightly. If they found out what was happening, there would be hell to pay and the Order wouldn't stop until they were satisfied that they had gotten proper vengeance. At the same time, however, Kyven felt that it was not just the Order who had the right to vengeance. Though there was nervousness deep in his belly when he thought about them finding out what Athan had done or what they were trying to find out, there was also a sense of responsibility and drive. More than ever now he wanted to know what happened to his father and was willing to face danger in order to avenge Aegeus the loss of his life, his mother the loss of her husband and the life that she should have lived, and himself and his brother the loss of their father and knowing who and what they really were.

The area around him was quiet and Kyven looked up, wondering where everyone else had gone. They had traveled for several hours and were nearing the Denynso compound when they had decided that it was time to stop and rest. The thrill of the incredibly fast travel had started to wear off, leaving exhaustion and hunger in its place, and Kyven reached into one of the bags that sat on the ground beside the fire and pulled out some of the food that they had brought along. He imagined that Maxim and Ivy had gone off on their own to talk through whatever had been happening between them in the last few days, and he hoped that they would be able to resolve it. He had never seen his brother as happy as he was with that woman, and now that he had found Emerie, he felt that he might be beginning to understand what Maxim was feeling.

That thought of Emerie brought a slight moment of panic to Kyven's heart and he stood, looking around as he realized that he had not seen her since they had stopped their vehicles and began to set up camp for the night. She had told him that she was going to go down to the small river that Athan said was nearby and bathe, but she had not yet returned and Kyven worried that something had happened to her in the time that she had been away. He didn't put it past the Order to capture the woman and use her as bait to lure the others to them. They wouldn't care that she was completely innocent in this matter and didn't even fully understand what was happening. They would care only that she was alone and vulnerable to them.

Athan approached from the other side of the fire carrying more brush to keep the flames going. His face changed when he saw Kyven's expression and he took a step toward him.

"Is everything alright?" he asked, his voice sounding concerned.

"Emerie hasn't come back," he said. "Maxim and Ivy are together wherever they are, but Emerie is alone."

"She said that she was going down to the river to bathe," Athan said.

"I know that," Kyven replied, sitting down to pull his boots back on as he prepared to go look for her. "She has been gone for a long time, though. What if the Order found her?"

"If the Order found her, we would already know about it," he said. "They have no use for her."

"They would know that if they had her, that I would come for her," he said, adjusting the knife attached around his hips.

"If they want us," Athan said, his voice becoming slightly gravelly as he spoke, "they will come for us. Go down to the river and look for her. I will go find Maxim and Ivy. We need to stay together as much as we can. Together we have much more of a chance against them or anything else that we may encounter here. We need to remember that this is no longer just a journey. We are not just exploring. The choices we have made are more dire than you might imagine now, but they are the ones that bind us. In their eyes we have gone rogue, and they have no tolerance for rebellion."

"Why would my father – or you – be a part of something so horrible?" Kyven asked.

"It wasn't always like this, Kyven. This is the brutality of war and the reality of deceit. The Order was always good. We fought, but it was for the protection of others. It only took the destruction of one heart to make that change."

"I don't understand."

"Everyone is fragile. Even if they won't admit it and even if they never show it, everyone is only strong enough to handle but so much. That time came and the Order changed, I believe that is what your father was fighting for, he wanted to restore what had been lost."

Athan dropped the brush to the ground and took a few steps backwards.

"Go," he said. "Find Emerie and bring her back here. From now on no one goes anywhere alone. We stay together at all times."

He turned and started away from the fire, his pace faster than what it had been when he approached Kyven just moments before. Something that Kyven had said had startled the older man, but he wasn't going to question it. Athan understand the Order and everything that they did on a level that Kyven and the others didn't. Even if he tried to explain it, they would never be able to truly understand it the way that he did. He had lived it, breathed it, and existed only within it for the vast majority of his life. Even though he wouldn't want to admit the connection, he shared heartbeat with the other members of the Order, a rhythm that controlled how they thought, felt, and responded to the world around them. The thought that those compulsions had become so twisted in some of their members had to be frightening for Athan, reminding him that he was always only a step away from becoming like them.

Kyven turned and ran toward the river, trying to remember the directions that Athan had given Emerie when she had asked. It shouldn't be far from the camp, and Kyven felt a surge of motivation when he heard the light sound of the bubbling water coming toward him from the darkness ahead. He continued at a faster pace, holding back the urge to call out her name. He didn't want to bring any more attention to himself than they already had just by settling in and building the fire. Finally the moonlight from overhead illuminated the surface of the water and Kyven felt relief wash over him as he saw Emerie walking through it. She was deep enough that the water came up nearly to her shoulders but he could see enough of her to know that she had undressed fully to submerge herself.

Her back was to him and as she moved her hair shifted, allowing the soft glow of the moon touch the smooth, pale skin of her back. She stretched her hands out to her sides, waving them slowly so that her fingertips just grazed across the surface of the water. Kyven felt struck by her. He paused where he was, several yards away from the bank of the river, and watched her as she continued to move gracefully through the night-darkened water. She looked so at peace, so calm as her body parted the water and allowed it to sweep across her skin. He didn't want to disturb her. In the time that he had known her she had seemed like she was holding something within herself, carrying a burden that she didn't want to share. Now as she bathed quietly in the river she seemed as though she had rested that burden on the bank and stepped into the water free from it, if only for a few moments.

The desire and adoration that he felt for her surged higher within him and he longed to be close to her. He knew that she had feelings for him. She had offered those feelings timidly, not going far enough to admit that she loved him and now allowing him close enough to her for him to show his love for her, and she had committed herself to coming along with him when he left the kingdom. Even though he knew that she didn't fully understand the implications of everything that was going on, he knew that she was aware that she was putting herself in danger just by agreeing to go with him. It put him in a strange and confusing place where he was at once ready to fully give himself over to her and unsure if she would ever be ready to do the same.

His need to be close to her overpowered any unsureness that he felt and Kyven walked slowly toward the edge of the water. He was nearly to the bank when Emerie turned. She gasped when she saw him, her arm coming up to cover her breasts even though they were not quite visible over the top of the water. Kyven held up a hand to calm her.

"It's just me," he said quietly.

"Kyven!" she said, not moving her arm away. "What're you doing? You scared me."

"I'm sorry," he said. "I didn't mean to intrude. I was worried about you when you hadn't come back and Athan said that I should come and find you."

"You didn't intrude," she said after a quiet moment.

She didn't look as startled now and she slowly lowered her arm away from her body. The water was high enough that only the top swell of her breasts was visible, but even that was enough to make Kyven ache for her. The water moved slightly, revealing more of her skin and all thoughts of Athan's warnings disappeared from his mind. Emerie was safe. The Order had not come for her and now they were peacefully alone at the water.

Kyven moved cautiously, removing his boots slowly. Emerie watched him and he knew that she was fully aware of his intentions. He wanted her to be. He wanted her to watch his every move and know exactly what he was doing so that she could control it if she wanted to. When she said nothing about his boots, Kyven took the hem of his tunic and pulled it off over his head. He saw her draw in a breath, her eyes grazing across his chest and stomach as she drank in the sight of him. Kyven paused for another brief moment and then released the ties on the front of his pants, easing them off without taking his eyes away from hr.

Now completely vulnerable to her, Kyven stepped forward. The cool of the water rose up to touch his toes and he felt a slight shiver move through his body. It was not as intense, though, as the shiver that she created within him and he continued forward, letting himself sink into the water as slowly as he could. Emerie watched him, her lips parting slightly. He could see her starting to tremble and wondered what emotions were causing the reaction. The water pressed in around his body, making his movements even more gradual as he made his way across the sandy bottom of the river toward her.

When he was finally only a few inches away, Kyven lifted one hand and lightly touched the side of her face. Emerie sighed softly and tilted her head to brush her face against his touch. He ran the pad of his thumb across her lips and felt her kiss it. The soft pressure of her lips brought a long exhalation from deep in his chest and Kyven took another step toward her. He rested his hand on her hip and reveled in the feeling of her bare skin beneath his palm. He applied pressure to her hipbone to pull her closer to him and felt the tips of her breasts brush against his chest.

"Kyven," she whispered softly.

He took his hand away from her hip and used it to gently lift her chin so that her face tilted up to his.

"Hmmm?" he murmured, bringing his lips down to hers in a soft kiss.

She sighed as she relaxed into the kiss, but then he felt her pull back from him. He looked at her and saw her shaking her head, looking down at the water and the arm that she had crossed over her breasts again.

"I can't," she said, her voice tight with emotion. "I'm sorry, Kyven. I can't do this."

Embarrassment rushed through him and he took a step back so quickly he nearly stumbled.

"I'm sorry," he said, looking away and turning around so that he could get back onto the bank and dress as quickly as he could.

When he turned back around she was several yards away from him, her back to him as she finished dressing. She straightened the bottom of her shirt and then crossed her arms, wrapping her hands around her upper arms and hanging her head slightly. Kyven could see her shoulders trembling and could hear the soft sounds of her crying. He finished dressing and approached her cautiously, breaking through the embarrassment and discomfort with his need to soothe her.

"Emerie?" he said carefully as he got close to her.

He wanted to rest his hand on her back, but didn't know if she would welcome the touch or it would only upset her even further. Instead he came up to stand beside her and ducked his head so that he could look at her better.

"I'm so sorry," she said through her tears before he was able to say anything.

"What's wrong?" Kyven asked. "Did I do something?"

Emerie shook her head and looked up at him. The moonlight touched her eyes, sparkling on the tears and illuminating the trails that they left on her cheeks as they fell. He reached up and brushed one of them away. He had touched her so similarly just moments before, but now the contact felt so different. He ached for her in a different way now, the pain centered on his desperate desire to find out what had happened to hurt her and do whatever he could to ease that pain.

"No," she finally said. "You didn't do anything. It's me."

"What do you mean?"

Emerie hung her head again and started to cry harder, bringing her hands up to cover her face. Her vulnerability suddenly made Kyven remember what Athan had said about them being alone.

"Come on," Kyven said. "Let's go back to the camp. Athan said that we shouldn't separate while we're out here."

Emerie nodded and allowed him to loop his arm around her shoulders and help her walk back toward the camp, supporting her as much as he could without feeling like he was overwhelming her with his presence. The others were around the fire when they got back. Emerie shied away from the light coming from the flames and after acknowledging them, rushed toward her tent muttering something about wanting to get to sleep so that they could get up early and finish their trip. Kyven walked to the edge of the fire and found the food that he had started to prepare sitting on a plate beside the pit. He took a bite of it but he was no longer hungry.

"Is everything OK?" Maxim asked.

Kyven looked at his brother, unsure of what to say.

"Everything's fine," he finally said. "I'm tired, too. I'm going to go to bed. Wake me up when you are ready to go."

He didn't wait for anyone to respond but went to his tent and ducked inside, closing the flap tightly. He changed his clothes and rested back on his bedroll, staring up at the top of the tent. Finally the others went to their own tents and the glow from the fire died. A few moments later he heard rustling outside of his tent.

"Kyven?"

Emerie's voice was startling but welcome in the darkness. He leaned forward and opened the tent, moving back so that she could come inside.

"Is something wrong?" he asked.

He felt like that question was becoming his default greeting, as though it was the first thing that his mind came up with when he saw another person. He wondered if there would ever be a time when that didn't happen, and hoped that it would come soon.

"I wanted to apologize again," Emerie said.

Kyven shook his head.

"You don't need to apologize," he said.

The truth was that he didn't want to think about the situation anymore. He didn't want to have to relive those moments any more deeply than he already was.

"Yes, I do," Emerie said, settling down on her knees on his bedroll as Kyven moved back to sit further up. "I need you to understand what happened."

"It's fine, Emerie."

"No, it's not," she insisted. "I care about you. I care about you so much, and that's why I need you to understand what happened back there."

"If you care about me so much, then why..."

"Because I'm married. At least, I was."

Kyven was startled by the revelation and he stared at her, unable to respond, willing her to continue so that she could clarify what she had said.

"When I left with the Nyx 23 mission, I was married. I believed, like everyone else on the mission, that we were only going to be gone for a short time. A few weeks, maybe. A couple of months at the very most. My husband was used to me going on missions, but he was nervous about this one. He didn't like that we were doing something so outside of the usual goals and actions of the department. He thought that it was dangerous and he asked me not to go. I told him that I had to, that I believed in what we were doing and that there was nothing to be worried about. I know that he was upset with me the morning that we left."

"What was his name?" Kyven asked.

"What?" Emerie asked, sounding surprised by the question.

"He had a name," Kyven said, remembering what Maxim had told him about his conversation with Athan and the older man's reluctance to speak Aegeus's name. "He deserves to be called by his name."

Tears came to Emerie's eyes and Kyven saw her lips tremble slightly.

"Jason," she said quietly.

The name came out of her mouth sounding powdery and hesitant, as if she hadn't said it in so long that her tongue wasn't sure how to form it any longer.

"How long were you married?"

"Just two years."

Kyven nodded. Hearing that she had spent years of her life with another man was painful and brought an uneasy, somewhat sick feeling to his stomach, but he couldn't pretend that it didn't exist. She had lived another life in another time, well before he was even born, and he couldn't simply act like it had never been. The man who she had devoted her life to then, Jason, had been precious to her and he had been there to care for her and protect her in every way that he could when she didn't even know that Kyven existed. He deserved respect for that.

"You've been thinking a lot about him."

He had meant it as a question but it came out as more of a statement, an acknowledgement of what she was suffering through. Emerie nodded.

"When I got on that ship there wasn't a single thought in my mind that I wasn't going to be getting back to him in just a short while and we would make everything fine again. It was just going to be another mission and then we would keep going with our lives together. We had a vacation planned for later in the year and had started talking about starting a family."

This revelation took the breath out of Kyven's lungs and he had to fight to keep himself from allowing the tears that were forming in his eyes to escape.

"I wish I had known," he said. "I'm sorry."

"There's no way for you to have known," she told him. "I didn't tell you and I should have. I have struggled with it since we woke up in the settlement. When we crashed he was my sense of connection back to Earth. I knew that he was there thinking about me and missing me and hoping that I was doing alright. I thought about him every day and it was what kept me going during those first really hard months. Finally I came to terms with the fact that we weren't going to get back to Earth, that our ship was destroyed beyond repair and that there was no way for anyone on Earth to know where we were or what had happened to us. I realized then that Jason must think that I was dead. For days I wondered what he was thinking about. I wondered if he had a funeral for me and if he was still living in the same home that we shared. I wondered about silly things like what he had done with my clothes and if he had ever painted the bathroom yellow like he had wanted to when we first moved in but I insisted that it stay white. Most of all I thought about his wedding ring."

"His ring?" Kyven asked, feeling confused.

"Yes. On Earth when we marry we exchange rings. I don't know if it's the same way with the Mikana."

"No," he told her. "That's not one of the rituals that we share with the humans."

Emerie held up her hand and for the first time Kyven noticed the thin gold band that she wore around her finger. It was so tiny, and yet its presence was intimidating.

"I kept wearing it the entire time we were in the settlement and I wondered how long he would wear his. To me, we were still married. Our relationship was just as real and just as committed as it had been the day that I got on that ship. I knew for him, though, it was different. He thought that I wasn't alive any longer. He had no reason to continue to think of us as married or to keep living his life as though we were. For years I tormented myself wondering when was going to be the day that he was going to take that ring off and start looking for a new partner. When was going to be the day that he was going to find someone else and start thinking of her the way that he thought of me. When was he going to get married again, when were they going to have a child? Even with those thoughts, though, I could never bring myself to think of our marriage as over. I was still just as much alive as I always had been, and that meant that my vows to him were still valid."

"I'm sorry," Kyven said again. "It was never my intention to offend you or to cross any lines."

He felt himself pulling away from her even in the small space, but she reached for him and rested a hand on his arm as if to hold him in place.

"That's the thing, Kyven. You didn't. I was on that settlement for 15 years before the Covra locked us. People age differently on Uoria than they do on Earth. I don't know how to explain it, but I know that I look and feel younger than those 15 years should have made me. Jason wouldn't. He would have aged just as he was going to. We married very young because of my intended career, but even with that, in those 15 years he would be older than you are now. His life would have been set. I know him." She took a breath. "I knew him. He still would have wanted a wife and children and the life that we had always imagined sharing. By the time that the Covra locked us, he would have had all of that. Our marriage was over to him, because he thought that I was gone. Then more than a century passed. I didn't change as I lay there, but again, he would have. He would have lived those years and they would have changed him, gradually fading him away until his life was over. He thought that I was dead when I didn't come back from that mission. I know that he is now. I don't know if he struggled with the idea of letting our marriage go and no longer thinking of me as his wife, but I know that I have been having a difficult time with it. The feelings I have for you are so strong, stronger than I would have ever thought that I would be able to experience again, and it is hurting me more than I could have imagined it would. I feel so guilty for feeling this way about you. I still feel loyal to Jason and to our marriage, and I'm scared that feeling these things for you is betraying him in some way."

"Emerie," Kyven said, taking her hands in his and pulling them up so that he could cradle them against his chest, "listen to me. It's alright. I would never want you to do anything that would make you uncomfortable or unhappy. You know that Jason has been gone for a long time. You also know that he would want you to be happy. No one could ever replace what he was for you. You can never expect to love anyone exactly the same way that you loved him. That doesn't mean, though, that you can't love someone else in their own way and let them love you in return. I will be respectful and patient for as long as you need me to. I have waited for you my entire life. I can wait longer. I want you to know, though, that I am not asking you to make a choice. There is no choice to be made. You don't have to decide to either keep loving him or to love me. One is loving your memories and one is loving your future. You know better than anyone that you can never predict what is going to happen in the next moment of your life. You can't live it thinking that you know and planning every breath around that, and you can't live it pretending that the past is still here with you. All you can do is just live."

2

―――

"Are you sure that you want to do this?" Lynx asked, stepping carefully around a sharply pointed rock that had risen out of the ground in front of him.

Rain was walking several feet ahead of him, her eyes fixed on the horizon, and he saw her nod.

"Yes," she said. "I have to. Avoiding a pile of metal and weeds just because there are some bad memories attached to them won't do anyone any good. I have to be able to do this for everyone on the team, even those who never made it out of the wreckage."

Her voice was tight with emotion and Lynx felt the urge to pick her up and carry her back to the settlement where he knew that she would be safe. The last time that they had gone to the wreckage was incredibly difficult for her, and then she had the distraction of convincing Pyra to let Maxim live so that they could bring him back to Creia. Now she didn't have that layer of protection that could keep her thoughts from wandering to the meaning of the scattered bones of the ship that had brought her and the rest of the team from Earth. Going there would mean that she was forced to come face-to-face with those memories again, reliving them a way that she hadn't in more than one hundred years.

They continued in silence for several more minutes and Lynx found his thoughts wandering to the rest of his clan. The Denynso warriors were a fiercely loyal people and had spent their entire lives together. It was simply the way of their kind. They lived, fought, and died on the compound. Things had changed so drastically in the past months that the clan was almost unrecognizable. Not only had they left the compound in search of greater understanding of the rest of Uoria and the types of creatures that inhabited the planet, but they were now scattered. They hadn't stayed together as they had all assumed that they would. When they first made the decision to leave and go on their mission, it had always been assumed that they would travel together and return together. Nothing really would change. They would find out what they needed to know, go back to their compound, and better their defenses for the possibility that they may someday come into battle with one of the species that they had found on their journey.

He wondered now as he walked through the tall grasses at the center of the land they had explored if that thought had been naïve. Could they have closed their eyes and their minds to the possibilities that were awaiting them on the other side of the wall that had contained them their entire lives? Maybe they should have realized that when they made the decision to change something so central to the way that they lived their lives, that they would be creating a ripple effect that would have implications for all other aspects and all other moments of their lives. Even as he thought about this, though, Lynx knew that he was just like the rest of the warriors. He hadn't wanted to think of a life that wasn't like the one that he anticipated from the time he was a child. He had been raised in the loyalty, duty, and tradition of the warriors and the idea of walking away from that life and willingly embarking on one that was so completely different was not something that he ever would have wanted to imagine. He knew that the others felt the same way and that they would never bring themselves to admit it.

Rather than being all together, protected in the compound that had always been their home but that they had only recently discovered was not where their clan had originated, they were spread across the planet and throughout the galaxy. Some had remained on the compound, others stayed in the settlement with those of the Nyx 23 project who decided that they wanted to remain on Uoria, others had traveled to the Mikana kingdom, and still others had taken the greatest adventure that Lynx could imagine and gone to Earth to be a part of Ty and Samira's wedding. Though part of him felt sad for not being with the others on Earth and experiencing the traditional wedding ritual of the humans, he knew that he had made the decision that was right for him. His mate had made the decision to remain on Uoria rather than returning to Earth, and his place was with her. If she ever changed her mind and decided that she wanted to visit her home planet, he would travel along with her. For now, though, she was committed to finding out more about why her mission had been diverted the way that it had and the actual events that had led up to them being stranded on Uoria at the mercy of the creatures that lived there.

Nothing around them looked familiar to Lynx, but soon he saw the faint outlines of pieces of wreckage in the distance. He had been to this place only once before, on that dismal afternoon when he stood behind Pyra and watched him stare down Maxim with hatred, fury, and fear in his eyes. Lynx had been terrified then. He had been afraid for Maxim's life and for the future of the interactions between the Mikana and the Denynso. He had been afraid that if Pyra had gone back on his word to Rain that she would completely turn her back on the Denynso and he would lose the mate that he loved so desperately. He had also been afraid that if he watched Pyra let the darkness that had appeared within him overtake his thoughts and killed Maxim as he threatened that he was going to, that he would lose the trust, faith, and respect that he had for the leader of the warriors. They were thoughts that were painful to bear then and that rushed back to him now as they approached what remained of the massive ship that had been state-of-the-art in its time but had been reduced to nothing but tattered steel and cast-aside components gradually being reclaimed by the planet.

Rain didn't hesitate when they approached the wreckage. Instead, she ducked down and walked right into the large opening that Lynx remembered led into what was left of the actual structure of the ship. Though she had told the others about what it had been like in those last moments on the ship and during the crash, she had been more reserved with them than she had been with him. For him she had reserved the most painful and graphic of the details, offering up memories that he had had to choke down and pretend that they didn't sear into his belly every time that he thought of them. He had spent his life preparing for war and surging into battle with the rest of the Denynso, yet what she had gone through had sent shivers along his skin. He couldn't imagine the terror that must have coursed through her when she realized that the ship was no longer under the control of the pilot and that they were headed for a planet that none of them had ever visited, that Earth didn't even know existed at the time.

In the quiet of their time alone together she had described what it had felt like when the ship began to hurtle toward the ground. She told him of turbulence that had made it nearly impossible to stand and had forced most of them into their seats. He could only imagine that most of them, if not all of them, were thinking that these were the last moments that they would ever live and were dreaming of the people they loved who they had left behind and who would never know what had happened to them. He wished he could take those thoughts from her, could remove the memories from her mind and replace them with happiness that would soothe the hurt that he knew still lingered there. At the same time, though, he would never ask her to forget who she was or where she came from. Those may be some of the most torturous of memories that he could imagine, but they were hers and that made them precious.

3

Rain knew that Lynx was behind her and it gave her the strength to continue into the remnants of the ship. She hadn't looked back at him during the last portion of the walk to the wreckage because she didn't want to see the emotion in his eyes. She knew that if she looked at him she would see the worry in his expression and it might chip away at the resolve that she had as she pushed through the grass and toward the site of the crash that had made Uoria, as much as she and the other members of the project hadn't anticipated or wanted it to be, her home.

Now that they were at the wreckage all she could think about was those last moments on the ship. She rested her hand on the wall beside her and closed her eyes, letting her senses come alive with the memories that swept over her in the space. She could remember the darkness that suddenly surrounded them as the power within the ship completely cut off over Uoria. It was darkness like she had never experienced, so deep and intense that she almost felt like she could reach out and scoop it into her hands and cast it away from her. The thoughts that had ran through her mind as they hurtled down into the unknown were fevered and terrifying. It felt as though everything had fallen out from beneath them and she had no idea what was going to happen in the next second.

Many of the crew had gone to their seats, strapping themselves in the way that they had as they prepared for launch and landing. For the first few moments Rain had sat in her seat the way that they had, but sitting there felt like she was even more out of control than she already knew that she was. She couldn't just sit there and allow whatever was going to happen to happen without trying to do something. She scrambled out of the chair and felt her way toward the pilot's cabin, using her memory of the ship to guide her through. The darkness around her seemed to amplify the screams of her crewmates, but she used them to fuel her forward, to push her ahead even through the fear that was building in her chest.

Her hand finally touched the hatch to the ship's control room and she pressed against it with all of the strength that she could, having to force it open because the power was not there to open it for her. She could see better in the control room by merit of the light filtering in through the wide, curved glass that covered the front of the ship, enabling her to see the outlines of what was inside. The pilot was sitting in his chair, his hands seemingly frozen over the controls. He didn't move as she approached and she felt her heart sink down into her stomach. A moment later the ship smashed into the ground and her body flew backwards, crashing into the wall and sliding to the floor. The screams stopped and there was a moment of intense, horrific silence.

A moment later the sounds returned, but they seemed to come to her through water. They were undefined and fuzzy, making it difficult to even understand where they were coming from or who they were. The impact of the crash had sent painful shocks through her body and she didn't feel like she could stand. Instead she began to crawl forward, using the faint light that was still coming through the front of the ship to guide her as she moved through the cabin. Sharp pain cut into her hands and she lifted them, watching as trails of blood slid across her palms and down her wrists. She forced herself to continue, moving toward the dark form on the floor that she knew was the pilot.

Rain touched the pilot's back, shaking him slightly to try to get him to respond to her. He didn't move and she shook him harder, still with no response. A sudden glow of green light filled the room and Rain turned toward the door to the room. Greyson stood in the doorway, blood streaming from a wound in his forehead and looking at her with wild eyes. The light stick in his hand gave her enough light that she was able to see that the pilot was crumpled, lying on his hip with his torso and face down on the floor. She grabbed hold of him and pulled until he rolled over and she could see his face. There was a large piece of glass embedded in his neck, but not enough blood trickled around it. Her breath came from her lungs in harsh, ragged gasps as she reached for the glass and touched it with her fingertips.

"Rain?" Greyson said from behind her.

"Rain?" He said it again and she heard his voice blend with Lynx's. "Rain?"

It grew louder and more insistent and she realized it was only Lynx calling out for her. Her eyes opened and she realized that she had lowered herself to her knees on the weed-covered floor of the destroyed control room. Her hands were rested exactly on the place where she had found the body of the pilot, his skin already far colder than it should have been when she touched him. She turned them over and looked at the faint white scars that marked her palms.

"Are you alright?" Lynx asked, coming to crouch down beside her.

She turned to look at him and saw the look of concern in his eyes that she had expected. Now that she saw it, though, she welcomed it. It started to fade the fear and sadness that had settled into her as the memories coursed through her mind. Knowing that he was there beside her comforted her and she nodded.

"Yes," she said. "I'll be fine."

"Did you find something?"

Rain looked back down at the floor, trying to decide whether she wanted to tell him about the memories that had just come over her. She wanted to share them, to take some of the burden off of herself by giving it over to him to bear, but at the same time she didn't feel like she couldn't bring herself to speak them. These were still hers to suffer, hers to bear, and it wasn't the time for her to release that yet.

"No," she said, shaking her head. "Not yet."

"Can you tell me why you wanted to come here? This isn't a happy place for you. It isn't a happy place for anyone."

"Exactly," Rain said.

"What?"

"This isn't a good place. There aren't happy memories here."

"I'm not understanding you," he said, straightening to his feet as she did.

Rain moved deeper into the ship, forcing thoughts of that day to stay away from her as she continued making her way over the wreckage.

"I haven't been able to stop thinking about what Ivy said."

"What did she say?"

"It's more what she didn't say. When she was talking about how the government on Earth responded to the team's disappearance and went to Penthos, something bothered me. It took me a while to realize it, but I figured it out."

"What?"

"What happened to the Valdicians and their prisoners?"

"What do you mean?"

Rain pushed a tangled piece of metal away with her foot and bent down to look into a large tear in the wall into what she remembered would be a corridor.

"I told you that the reason that we went on this mission was because the Valdicians had an illegal prison compound on the previously unexplored planet. That was not a minor infraction. You have to remember that this was a long time ago. This was when intergalactic cooperation was still in very early days. There was still a tremendous sense of suspicion and uneasiness, and the agreements and laws that had been put into place had been chosen specifically to create security and control. The fact that the Validicians had gone against those laws so blatantly would have made them a target. I would assume that the military would come in and kill off all of the Validicians."

"Maybe they did."

Rain tore away weeds and vines that had grown over the gap and crouched down further to move through the wall into the corridor. It was no longer intact. She remembered her own hands pulling away the pieces of steel so that they could use them to build their settlement. There were only fragmentary reminders of the shape of the ship, allowing her to follow it as if walking through those memories that she had tried so hard to keep out of her mind.

"No," she said, shaking her head. "They would know. It

would have been one of the first things that she would have told us. With a military maneuver that big there would be a statue or a holiday or a museum or something. They wouldn't just do nothing. It doesn't make sense that they wouldn't have done something to acknowledge the loss of our team and the heroic actions of the military if that is what had happened."

"You said that the cooperation between the planets and the species were still tenuous at that time," Lynx said. "What if Earth didn't want to say anything about that type of mass killing because they didn't want to get a bad reputation? Showing that this type of activity could go on and that it took that level of force to stop it, and could be used as proof that there shouldn't be any kind of federation, that all of the planets and the species should keep to themselves."

"Alright," Rain said, reaching a section of grass that would have been where two corridors would have crossed. "I may be able to accept that as an explanation for the Validicians, but what about the prisoners?"

"What do you mean?"

"It doesn't make sense that there is no mention of the prisoners or what happened to them. Earth has a habit of making memorials and honoring the innocent dead in lasting, highly visible ways. But they also have a habit of saving people. What happened to those prisoners? Where did they go?"

Something suddenly triggered in her mind and she spun around, trying to orient herself, willing her mind to build up the walls of the ship again so that she could see where she was and navigate her way through it to the specific room that she needed to find.

"What if there weren't any prisoners left by the time that the military got there?"

"No," Rain said, increasing her pace as she made her way through the overgrown wreckage toward a section that would have once been the largest, most important dormitory in the ship. "That would have likely caused even more of an issue. If the Valdicians had killed off everyone and the military found that when they got to Penthos, it wouldn't have mattered if they were trying to keep up appearances or gloss over what had happened. There would be something. Everyone would know that that had happened. There was nothing."

She found the area of the wreckage that she knew had been the pilot's personal quarters and began to dig through what was left. They had shied away from clearing out this area of the ship after burying the pilot. Even though they probably could have used more of the metal and components that they left there to build more in their settlement, but none of them felt right about dismantling the space that had been so private in the pilot's life. The loss of their leader had been devastating, and Rain knew that only she had been there to see what had happened to him. Only she knew that he had already been gone long before the ship crashed into the ground.

"What are you doing?" Lynx asked as she dug through the wreckage.

"I need to find the box."

"What box?" he asked.

"The pilot's box. Every pilot had a secure box that they kept in their quarters. It's where they kept all of their records and most valuable personal possessions. It was never recovered when we dismantled the ship. I hadn't thought about that until now. It might have something in it that will help us understand what happened."

4

The Denynso compound looked quiet and empty as they approached it and for a moment Maxim felt a sense of fear ripple through him. He didn't know what threats still lingered on the planet for the Denynso, and now that he knew more about the Order and what they had done in the past, he found himself afraid that someone had made a link between the Mikana and the Denynso and come for them.

The group brought their vehicles over the wall and landed, concealing them as much as they could in the trees. It felt strange climbing out of the vehicles and looking around himself realizing that they were in the territory of the Denynso without the accompaniment of even one of the warriors. He looked over at Athan and saw dark emotion brewing in his eyes. There was pain there that the older man wasn't putting voice to, and Maxim could only begin to imagine what he was thinking and feeling. From what he had learned from Creia in his first visit to the compound, if Athan had come here before, it would not have been when the warriors were living there, but when it was Loralia's kind who inhabited the beautiful land.

They walked through the trees toward the center of the compound with Maxim and Ivy leading those who had not been with them on the first visit. He reached beside him and took Ivy's hand. He had a rush of thankfulness for her presence in that moment. He loved her with an intensity that went beyond what he could have ever thought was possible, and the time that they had spent apart had only reaffirmed that for him. The touch of her hand gave him comfort now, and he allowed himself to feel reassured by knowing that she had spent more time in the compound and with the Denynso than he had. He was willing now to give himself over to trusting her. Despite loving her from the moment that he saw her, he had struggled within himself to completely make her a part of his journey. He knew that it was because of the loss of his father, the instability within him that came from the years of watching his mother try to navigate living her life without her husband by her side. He never wanted to feel that. As deeply and desperately as it had hurt him to think of a time when he would not share his days and his nights with Ivy, he had forced himself to keep that thought in the back of his mind. He told himself that if he believed she was a tentative presence in his life, something that could at any moment leave, he wouldn't learn to rely on her.

When she began to question his motivations for seeking out an explanation behind his father's disappearance and the actions of the Order, it seemed that he had come to the point that he had dreaded. He had released her so that she would feel like it was easy for him, so that it would seem that it was of little consequence and she could simply go back to the life that she had, had before she had met him. In reality it had felt like he was tearing his very soul from within him, separating a part of himself from the rest of his being. Now he knew that she had be inextricable from him from the moment that they met and that no amount of telling himself that she was not so precious to him would prove it. Instead he was putting himself in the very position that he had been fighting to avoid. Rather than protecting himself from a life of trying to find meaning in a reality without his partner he was creating that very reality for himself. As soon as she was back in his arms, it was as though the air had returned to his lungs. In that moment he knew that he had no choice but to give himself over to her, to accept that she was a part of him and that he would have to trust in everything that they meant to one another.

They moved through the woods as quickly as they could and Maxim was relieved when he heard voices coming from the edge of the trees. He could see the sun on the other side of the shade just before he noticed the three Denynso women standing beneath the first tree of the woods. They each had baskets tucked against their hips and were gathering fruit from the trees. The women looked up at him as they approached and he saw them take several steps back, their faces registering nervousness. One looked to Ivy and seemed to relax slightly as recognition took hold.

"Hello," Ivy said. "Please don't be afraid. Everything's still alright. Do you know where Creia is?"

The women exchanged glances and then looked back at Ivy.

"He isn't here," one of them said, sounding as though it confused her that they didn't know the king was not at the compound.

"What do you mean he isn't here?" Ivy asked. "Where is he?"

"We don't know," another of the women said. "He didn't tell any of us where he was going. Theia told us at breakfast one morning that he had left but should be back soon."

"When was this?" Maxim asked.

The first woman seemed to think for a few moments.

"A few days ago," she told him. "Is there something wrong?"

Maxim didn't understand why, but the response started a slightly panicked feeling within him. Without saying another word he rushed the rest of the way out of the woods and continued toward the center of the compound. He needed to get to the main hall and talk to Theia. Maybe the women had misunderstood what she had said. If nothing else, they needed to know where the king had gone and why he had chosen to wait until the warriors and humans had left the compound to do it.

WHEN THEY FINALLY MADE IT to the main meeting hall they found Theia sitting in her chair, staring across the room as if completely lost in thought. When the guard announced their arrival she looked at them with an expression of hope blended with worry.

"Maxim," she said, standing and coming to the edge of the platform so that she could take his and Ivy's hands in greeting. "It's good to see you."

"It's good to see you, too, Theia," Maxim said. "This is Athan, my brother Kyven, and Emerie," he introduced, gesturing to the rest of the group.

The queen of the Denynso compound acknowledged each of them with a small nod and then turned her attention back to Maxim.

"Have you heard from Creia?" she asked. "Did he by chance come to your kingdom?"

Maxim felt confused and shook his head.

"No," he told her. "Where did he go?"

Theia looked panic-stricken. She gestured for them to draw closer to the platform.

"Please," she said, lowering her voice, "come with me. I need to speak with you but I don't want anyone else to hear."

The group followed her back around the platform to a spiral staircase that led up to what Maxim could only imagine were her and Criea's private quarters. They entered a lushly decorated room and she closed the door behind them, covering it with a thick tapestry. It seemed like an odd feature, but with everything he was learning about the ways of the planet before he was born and the types of conflicts that existed between the species unfurling before him with every new detail, he could understand the suspicion and caution that went into it.

"Soon after your group returned to the settlement to release those being held and the others left for Earth, Creia told me that there was something that he needed to do. He said that he was feeling guilty for not telling the warriors everything about the origin of our clan and our interactions with some of the other species of Uoria, and that it was time that he fixed everything, but in order to do that he needed to know more. I asked him not to go. I told him that I was scared and that I didn't think that he should be doing this."

"Have you had any communication with him since he left?" Ivy asked.

Maxim knew that the Denynso had the ability to communicate within their bonded pairs simply through their thoughts, enabling them to stay connected to one another even when they were not in the same area. This allowed them to share with one another without others hearing and kept them from being completely distanced from each other, even if they were miles apart. This should mean that Theia had been able to keep in contact with her mate while he was gone and would know where he was. The fact that she had asked them if they had seen him sent a shiver down Maxim's spine.

"No," Theia responded, the emotion making her voice crack. "He has only communicated with me once since he left. I've been trying to connect with him since he's been gone and I haven't been able to. I don't know what to do."

"What did he say when he communicated with you?" Maxim asked.

Theia looked at him with terror in her eyes, the tears trickling down her face and across her lips.

"Badlands."

Maxim felt his body tighten and the fear contract his heart. He remembered what Creia had said about the badlands. These were where his family had lived and where the clan had begun. They were also the site of some of the most brutal fighting that Maxim had ever heard about, fighting that forced half of the clan away and destroyed the other. He knew that if Creia had ventured into the badlands on his own and was not communicating with Theia, there was something wrong.

"We need to get to him," Maxim said. "We have to find him and make sure that he is alright. We're going to need to be able to communicate with Theia while we're gone."

"How?" Ivy asked. "None of us can communicate with each other the way that the Denynso can."

"Maybe one of the couples here on the compound can help us," Theia suggested. "Not all of the warriors left on the shuttle. Some are still here with their mates."

"Call the one you trust the most here. It is very important that he is completely loyal and trustworthy. No one else must know where Creia is or what might have happened to him."

Theia nodded and swept out of the room.

"Do you think that this is going to work?" Ivy asked.

Maxim reached over and took her hand, squeezing it tightly. He didn't want to respond. The truth was he didn't know how to. He could only hope that they were going to be able to find a way to communicate because he knew that he had to find Creia but didn't know what they were going to encounter when they left the compound for the badlands.

Several minutes later Theia came back into the room with two Denynso Maxim didn't recognize. Both looked apprehensive, obviously uncomfortable to be in the private space of the king and queen, a place where none of the Denynso had ever been permitted, even the sons of the king and queen themselves. They were permitted into other spaces of the monarch's quarters, but these rooms had always been reserved only for the couple so that they could have peace and protection only for them away from all of the pressures of their station.

Theia came around the pair and gestured for them to sit. The two stayed close together as they walked further into the room and then settled into place on the cushioned stool on the other side of Ivy. They exchanged glances and Maxim saw them holding hands tightly.

"Thank you for coming," Theia said. "This is Maxim, Ivy, Kyven, Emerie, and Athan. Please meet Nylek and his mate Mina."

The group exchanged half-hearted greetings and Nylek and Mina turned their attention back to Theia, looking at her expectantly.

"What can we do for you, Queen?" Nylek asked carefully.

Theia looked at Maxim.

"Please," she said.

He was stunned at the imploring sound in her voice. This woman was meant to be the strongest of the Denynso clan, and yet she looked frightened and almost as though she was fading away from them. He stood and turned so that he was looking at the pair.

"Before I continue I need to know that you understand that by coming here you are agreeing to be held under the strictest of confidences. Nothing that we discuss here or even the fact that you were asked to come here will be shared with anyone outside of this room. It is of the utmost of importance that you abide by that, and I can assure you that I will hold it to the strictest of adherence."

"We understand," Nylek said.

Maxim looked at Mina and she nodded, leaning slightly closer to her mate as she did it. He knew that they were likely confused and possibly even scared, but he didn't have the time or the patience to comfort them in this moment. He knew that Creia's safety, and possibly his life, rested in the balance and them being able to find him as quickly as possible was essential. It was not just about Creia. What the king knew and his connections with the history of Maxim's kind could make a tremendous difference in the fulfillment of his quest to understand what happened to his father. He could only press forward and pull those that he needed along with him, hoping that he could achieve what he needed to.

"The king may be in danger," he said. Their eyes widened, but he didn't pause for them to ask any questions. "I do not have the time to divulge the specific details. I can only tell you that he has left the compound in an effort to better understand his past and he may have found himself in a very treacherous situation. He has not been in communication with Theia for the majority of his time away and we have reason to belief that his life could be in imminent threat. My group will be leaving as soon as possible to hopefully find him and bring him back safely. In order to do that, however, we will need to remain in communication with the compound. I have asked that Theia select the warrior who she felt would be the most trustworthy to assist us in this mission and she chose you."

"What is it that you need me to do?" Nylek asked, standing.

"I ask that you come with us. Mina will stay here with Theia. Whenever there is need for us to communicate with Theia, you will send the message to Mina, who will relay it to Theia. The reverse will apply if Theia finds out something and needs to share it with us. You will be managing the most sensitive and confidential of information, so I trust you understand the importance of remaining discreet."

"Yes," Nylek said. "I would be honored to serve my king and queen this way."

He extended his hand to Maxim, who gripped it.

"Thank you, Nylek. I appreciate your service."

"Nylek," Theia said, stepping forward. "You will follow Maxim as you would Pyra or Creia himself. He has my full trust."

"I will, Queen."

"When will you leave?" Theia asked. "Will you stay the night?"

"No," Athan said. "That is too long."

"I agree," Maxim said. "We will stay here for a few hours to rest and replenish our supplies from our last trip and then we'll leave. We need to get to Creia as soon as we can."

5
———

Pyra stepped into the doorway of the bedroom and leaned against the doorframe to watch Eden as she put Lysander to bed. The room was shadowy, lit only by a small lamp on the nightstand that created a halo of light around her as she leaned over the crib and whispered to their infant son. He knew that this was a moment that he wanted to hold onto for the rest of his life. In all of the turmoil and pain that he had experienced in the past weeks, this treasured moment alone made him feel at peace.

Eden straightened and he crossed the room, gently placing a hand on her back. She knew his touch and wasn't startled by it, which brought an even greater sense of warmth to his chest. Even though he had spent his life waiting for the time when he would find his mate, he never would have imagined how it would have changed his existence. He knew that his parents loved each other deeply, but it wasn't until he had met Eden that he really understood what that meant. He never would have allowed himself to imagine the incredible dichotomy of emotions that filled him when it came to Eden and to their child, a child that he never thought would exist.

At once he felt a softness and tenderness that was totally foreign to him. From the time that he was old enough to understand, he was trained in the ways of the warriors. He was born to fight and to defend, and there was no secret throughout the galaxy that the Denynso took this responsibility very seriously. They were not kind when in battle and they showed little tolerance for any who crossed their paths. He was stern and fearsome, yet when she came into his life Eden had shown him that there was a place inside him that was completely vulnerable, if only to her. She could make him feel as though he was completely in her control with only a smile and the touch of her hand had more power on him than the mightiest of weapons that he had ever encountered on the battlefield. The arrival of their son had only brought a greater sense of gentleness and love. The fact that these two beings were tied to him in a way that was completely unchangeable, that even with the fear that she faced Eden was completely at ease with him, was at once empowering and humbling.

On the other hand, the vulnerability and tenderness that he felt when he was near his mate and child seemed also to intensify the feelings of defensiveness and aggression within him. The thought of anyone hurting them in any way infuriated him to a level that was almost unfathomable. In those moments when he felt that either of them was being threatened the world around him became hazy and everything that he saw was edged in red. He struggled to contain himself and he knew that in a single moment he could kill and never think about it again.

That tension was with him now as he curled Eden close to him and turned to kiss her head. The vantage point that his height gave him allowed him to see that even in her pajamas she was wearing the necklace that he had designed for her before the warriors first left the compound. It had been only weeks and yet it seemed a lifetime ago that they had made the decision to step over that boundary wall and see what else laid on the planet of Uoria. It seemed so long ago that he almost couldn't remember the day, just a few weeks before that, when he had met with Jem to design the necklace so that he could make it for Eden.

Just thinking about the friend that he had lost in what he thought was the final encounter that he would ever have with the Klimnu brought the pain and anger back in fresh waves. He had seen death on the fields before, of course. He could not have been a true warrior without knowing the taste and sight of blood, both that he drew and that was drawn from those who had stood beside him. Death among the Denynso was not common, however, and the way that Jem had died had been so much more painful than the deaths of any of the other warriors that he had seen. He did not run into battle and get struck down by another as he fought. He gave himself into death. He offered himself to it, ensuring that he grabbed hold of the last of the Klimnu and took them with him.

As Pyra stared at the pendant on the necklace, the piece of carefully hone metal that represented him cradling his mate and their child in his hand, he wondered if he had been wrong to encourage the other warriors to leave the compound. Their home planet had been a strange and forbidden mystery to them, but they had broken through the bonds of tradition that had held them within the compound and now the world was open to him, but he wasn't completely confident that it was the decision that he should have made. They had learned so much and ensured that at least most of the people in the Nyx 23 settlement survived. At the same time, though, he had caused pain and torment to the Mikana and now there was turmoil on the planet and within his own kind that hadn't existed before. Though he was glad that they had been able to help those that they had, he hoped that it was worth the damage that he felt like he had caused.

Eden let out a sigh and looked up at him.

"What is it?" he asked, stroking her cheek with his thumb.

"I can't stop thinking about Ryan."

"I don't think that he's going to be bothering you again after our conversation in the lab."

"I don't know, Pyra," she said, sounding nervous. "I think more than ever that he is capable of far more than anyone will give him credit for. You saw how he was. There is something going on. He is doing something and it's scaring the hell out of me." She sighed and looked down at the baby again. "And I can't get that picture that Simran and Jane showed us out of my mind."

"Why?" he asked.

She looked back up at him and shook her head slightly.

"There's something about it that really bothers me."

"What?"

"I don't know really. There's just something about it that seems off. I know that that big man in it is Denynso. At least partly."

"What do you mean 'partly'?" he asked, not liking the way that that word sounded.

"Like Lysander," Eden said.

"You are Denynso," Pyra argued. "You have been since Ciyrs healed you."

"I know," she said, "but is he? I didn't carry completely

like a Denysno, but I didn't carry completely like a human, either."

"What are you saying, Eden?"

"We had no way of monitoring how he was growing when I was pregnant with him, so we had no way of knowing how big he was or how developed. We didn't even really know when I got pregnant. What if I got pregnant with him our first time together, before I was changed?"

Pyra struggled enough with the memory of her being nearly killed by a Klimnu who came into the compound. The thought that it was not just Eden, but that she was also carrying their tiny son within her at the time of the attack made the rage soar inside him so that he felt like it was swelling in his muscles and tearing through his skin. He fought with himself to remain calm. His mate was obviously having difficulty with the situation and he didn't want to upset or frighten her any further. It was his responsibility to guard and support her, not to allow his emotions to overtake him.

"What would that have to do with the picture?" he asked.

"If we conceived Lysander during our bond that would mean that I was still fully human when it happened. Ciyrs would have changed me when I was already pregnant. I became Denynso but that doesn't change that the baby would have been made half of human and half of Denynso."

"I still don't understand."

"It means that it's possible, Pyra. It means that Lysander might not be full Denysno, which is proof that the two species can have a child together."

"So that man in the picture may look slightly different not because he is not Denysno, but because he is human as well."

"Yes, and that frightens me."

"Why?"

"Because that means that anything is possible. Everything that we know about the Dneynso and the humans is wrong. What does that mean for Uoria? Or just for the future of the species?"

Eden looked worn and scared and Pyra felt his heart aching for her. He hated to see her this way. He glanced down at his son and saw that he was sleeping peacefully, and then took Eden's hand and started leading her out of the room.

"Where are we going?"

"Just come with me," he said.

They walked together through the quiet house, moving carefully so as not to wake the others who were sleeping in the other bedrooms, and out into the back yard. Pyra had never seen anything like it and had been immediately fascinated when he first arrived at the house that had been set aside for them to live in during their time on Earth. On Uoria the homes were built very close together and had no barriers between them. While the outer portions of the compound were lush and rich, the center had been cleared out before they built their homes and main buildings, creating an expanse that was largely flat dirt and carefully mapped roads. This simplified and streamlined the area, but it did somewhat take away from the beauty that lay beyond. Here, though, the homes were much larger and further apart. Even the modest home where they were staying was considerably larger than the average warrior house and each had its own little segment of land that was partitioned off from the others with tall fences that did not permit those living on either side of the home to access or even see into it. Within this confine was soft green grass and towering trees, meticulously organized gardens of flowers and playthings that had once belonged to children who had lived there.

Pyra had been wary of the lawn when he first saw it. He appreciated the open, cooperative nature of the compound and the way that the closeness of the buildings connected all who lived there. After spending time in the grass and feeling the quiet peacefulness that came from being on the private section of land, though, he realized that he also very much valued that occasional time to be on his own and to not have to always live up to the outward behaviors and appearances that were expected of him. He could simple breathe and not have to think of anything but what was happening right there with him. He didn't know how he would feel about always being separated from everyone else and having the members of the clan isolate themselves rather than spending more time together as it seemed that many humans on Earth did. For the time of their visit, however, he was going to enjoy the lawn, and that started with spending some time in it with Eden.

Eden seemed to curl into herself slightly as they walked across the moonlight-dappled grass. She looked to either side of herself, wrapping the hand that wasn't holding Pyra's around her arm as if to cover herself.

"It's alright," he said to her. "It's just us out here. No one can see you."

Eden nodded and smiled up at him. They continued until they reached a thick tree that had slats of wood nailed along its trunk. Pyra released Eden's hand and started climbing up the pieces of wood. When he was nearly to the top he turned and glanced down at Eden, who stared up at him with a look of confusion on her face.

"What are you doing, Pyra?" she asked.

"I'm going up to the treehouse," he told her.

"What?" Eden said with laughter in her voice.

"Samira told me that human children like to play in these. I've never seen one before and I want to explore it."

"It's just a tree house Pyra," she said. "It's just a big wooden square with walls."

"I want to see."

Eden chuckled and started up the slats of wood behind him. Pyra continued until he reached the gap in the side of the treehouse that served as the door and slid his way inside. His shoulders barely fit and for a moment he was worried that he was going to get stuck and he was going to have the embarrassment of having to send Eden to get one of the other warriors so that he could help Pyra get out of the treehouse. Fortunately he made his way into the small space and was able to move out of the way for Eden to join him.

The inside of the treehouse was much too small for Pyra to actually stand up, but he was able to sit and lean back against the wall, curling his legs in to give Eden the room to come inside.

"We shouldn't stay out here very long," Eden said. "Lysander might need us."

"He's asleep," Pyra reassured her, "and if he does wake up and start crying one of the others in the house will hear him. He will be just fine."

He reached for her and pulled her into his arms, positioning her in his lap and cradling her against his chest. He tilted his head back and saw a rope tied from the center of the ceiling to a hook on the wall.

"What's that?" he asked.

Eden looked at it and shrugged.

"I don't know."

Filled with curiosity, Pyra reached up and unwound the

rope from the hook, giving it a hard tug. A section of the ceiling came down, opening up so that they could look up through the branches of the tree to the stars scattered above them.

"Did your treehouse when you were young have that?" Pyra asked.

Eden laughed softly.

"I didn't have a treehouse when I was young," she told him.

"You didn't?"

Pyra was beginning to truly recognize the variations that existed in the lives of human children on Earth. On the compound on Uoria lives were incredibly similar. Children had specific callings from birth and they discovered them fairly early. It was obvious who was meant to be a warrior and who would take on other roles within the clan, like Ciyrs the healer and Ty the baker and nurturer. When they were not training for those positions, they played in much the same ways. Since the clan was extremely cooperative in most ways, at least until the young warriors got old enough to begin feeling their strong urges toward the women and may choose to separate themselves in order to wait for their mate, there was little sense of those who had a lot and those who had little. Even he, the most powerful son of the king and queen, played with all of the other children and maintained a life virtually indistinguishable from theirs. The only real difference is that until he was old enough to be on his own he slept in the family quarters of the meeting hall. The realization that there were major differences in the opportunities and realities of the children of Earth made him sad and he was more thankful than ever that his own son was born and would be raised on their home of Uoria.

"No," Eden replied. "I didn't spend much time at home

when I was a child. Most of the time I was with my grand-mother and she didn't have trees in her yard that were big enough for us to build a treehouse. Even if she had, I'm not sure how we would have built one."

"Didn't you ever want to know what it was like to play in one?" he asked.

"Oh, I played in some of my friends'," she told him. "Not everyone had one, but the ones who did would usually invite groups of us over and we would play these elaborate games. That all pretty much ended by the time that we were eleven or twelve, though."

"What happened after that?"

"We just got too old for the games. Then people started using their treehouses for other reasons."

Eden giggled but Pyra didn't understand. He gave Eden a questioning look and she smiled at him.

"The girls used to bring their boyfriends up into their treehouses when they wanted to spend some time with them without their parents knowing," she explained.

Pyra was still getting used to the human concept of dating, but he caught on to what she was saying and imme-diately felt his stomach tighten in the way that it had since the moment that he sensed his mate was on her way to him.

"So you never got to do that?" he asked, running his hand up her back and feeling the slight ripples of her spine beneath the soft fabric of her pajamas.

"No," she said.

She sounded slightly breathless and he knew that she was feeling the same thing that he was. He ran his fingers along the back of her neck and around her shoulder so that he traced the neckline of her shift.

"Did you ever wish that you got to?" he asked.

"I never had anyone that I wanted to do it with."

"How about now?" he asked. "Can I make up that memory for you?"

Eden nodded and Pyra bent forward, capturing her mouth with his. It suddenly felt as if all of the tension and stress within him broke and he was able to completely lose himself in the feeling of her lips on his and her hips rolling subtly into his lap. He used the tip of his tongue to coax her mouth open and delved in, tasting her full as he used his hands to gather the hem of her long pajama shirt up her thighs and over her hips. As he did that Eden pulled at the ties on the front of his pants, releasing them so that she could free the erection that was pressing up toward her, aching for her.

She ran her hand adoringly along the length of him, applying just enough pressure that it sent waves of incredible sensation through him without pushing him too close to the edge. The combination was intoxicating and Pyra felt himself getting dizzy with his need for her. Eden had worn nothing beneath her pajama shirt and he could already feel the wet heat from her body pressing against his. He took her by her hips and lifted her, bringing her up so that he could enter her. She moaned as she settled back into his lap, taking him fully into her so that their bodies melded completely. Pyra leaned forward and touched his lips to the soft skin above the neckline of her shirt. Tucking his hands behind the small of her back he led Eden's hips into a deep rocking motion that kept him fully inside her but let him feel the intense sensation of her warm, tight walls massaging against his length.

Eden's head fell back and she let out a deep groan, her hands coming to Pyra's shoulders so that she could grip him as she picked up the rhythm of his hands. Pyra brought one of his hands around her hips so that he could use the pad of his thumb to stroke the taut pearl of flesh at her peak. The touch of his hand seemed to send her nearly out of control. She cried out and rolled her hips with greater insistence, at once pressing against his hand and driving him deeper inside her. Pyra had wanted to hold off, making their time together last, but he knew that he wasn't going to be able to control himself. He tightened his grip on her hip with one hand and continued to massage her with his thumb as he thrust up into her in a harder, faster rhythm.

He could feel his climax rushing upwards and he pulled her forward, crushing his mouth down on hers so that he could roar into their kiss as he poured into her. Eden gasped against his mouth, her fingers grinding down into his shoulders as he felt her squeeze him then contract around him in a series of pulses that pulled him deeper and drew each drop of him into her body. Finally their mouths parted and they panted against each other's shoulders, cradling each other in their arms as they let the preciousness of their reality together distract them, if only for a few moments, from the turmoil that existed just beyond that simple treehouse that they had made their fortress.

6

____

Creia felt like the life was slowly draining out of him and he fought to resist it. The room around him was dark and he could feel the table beneath him moving as it propped him up again, bringing him back to the position that had become so painfully familiar. He knew that in moments the hooded creature would come back and attach him again to the screen that would show him the strange laboratory room. He didn't understand the purpose of the ritual. The scene barely changed each time that he was forced to stare at it for hours. The only thing that he ever noticed that seemed to change was the position of the creature in the tube in the corner. There were days when it slumped and hung from its binds in such a way that Creia wondered if it was still alive. There were other times when it strained and thrashed, fighting against the chains with an almost terrifying fury.

As he waited for the screen to take its place in front of his eyes, Creia wondered when the last time that he ate was. The hooded being had come into the room a few times and poured water down his throat, but hadn't fed him.

Consciousness came to him randomly and without him knowing how long he had been awake or asleep so he didn't know how long he had been held captive. He could feel the weakness coming over him, however, and knew that he wouldn't be able to struggle much more. He had stopped fighting against the screen. His only hope was to conserve the strength that he did have so that he would have the best chances if he did happen to have the opportunity to get out of his binds and come up against the hooded creature, possibly allowing him to get out of wherever he was.

A moment later the hooded creature stepped into the room again and Creia gave himself over to having the screen attached to his head. The laboratory appeared in front of him again and he scanned it with his eyes to see if anything had changed. At first there was nothing different that he could see and he wondered if he was going to have to sit there and stare at the unchanging space again for several more hours still not understanding the purpose. After a few moments, however, the space changed. He noticed a long shadow cross the floor and the creature in the tube in the corner visibly stiffened. Creia strained to see who may have come into the room and a moment later saw a man in a stark white coat appear in his field of vision. The man at first acted like he didn't even realize that Creia was watching him. He moved around the space repositioning tubes and vials on the tables, then crossed to the creature in the back and slammed his hand against the thick glass that contained it. Creia saw the creature pull away from the glass as if startled by the sound.

The man laughed and then turned, looking directly at Creia. The king felt his eyes burning into him in a way that sent a tremor down his spine. The man approached slowly and gave Creia a vile, disturbing smile.

"Hello, king," he said, the last word have a distinct edge of disdain. "So kind of you to accept my invitation."

"Who are you?" Creia forced through his tight, dry throat.

Just the effort that it took for him to say that made him feel weaker and he could see spots bursting in his vision.

"Don't worry about that," the man said. "You don't need to know who I am. All that matters is that I know who you are and that I finally have you."

"What do you mean?"

"I have been so patient," the man said, the image of his face coming even closer. "I have waited so long and now, I finally have what I have been waiting for. It has been years. Years of my life that I have spent wanting to pay homage to my family and finish what they started. There were times when I was so frustrated, so angry. I felt like I may never actually succeed. I always thought that I was going to be the one who was going to be able to make my family proud. You see, they worked so hard. They were revolutionaries who were never accepted and respected the way they should have been in their time. Do you know how much that tormented me? How much I hated finding out that these incredible men who saw the world in a way that no one else did and could have completely changed the entire universe were shunned because of their brilliance? I didn't want that to continue. Even though they went to their graves knowing that their lives' work had not ever been fulfilled and that the scientific community had never found the place for them that they deserved, I was going to fix it. I was going to be the one who picked up where they left off and finished it."

"I don't understand."

"You don't need to. It has taken more work than you could ever imagine to finally get you here, but I managed it all. I will admit, though, I did almost lose faith for a short time. I thought that I had everything so perfectly planned out. I knew...I just *knew*... that everything was going to work out perfectly when I sent Eden to Uoria for her research."

"*Ryan,*" Creia growled, feeling a surge of anger flow through him as he realized that the face of the man in front of him was that of the man who Eden had described to him as being such a source of torment to her.

Ryan gave a malevolent laugh.

"I see no introductions were really needed. My reputation already precedes me."

"Where is Eden?" Creia asked.

"I don't know where she is," Ryan said. "For now. You see, I had this all planned out. It was all planned out. Eden didn't want to play nice with me when she was here. I could have made her a part of all of this and it would have been incredible. She would have had a life that she could never have imagined. It would have been amazing. Instead, she pushed me away. I didn't like that. For a while I was really upset about it. I wondered what it was that I did wrong and I let it really get to me. Suddenly, though, I realized that she had actually given me an opportunity. She had made it so much easier for me to get what I wanted. I told her that she would go to your compound and collect the blood of the most powerful of the Denynso warriors and then return here. Of course, I knew that that was not ever going to happen. Everyone knows how closely guarded you are and how aggressively you defend the blood of your kind. I knew that she would go and as soon as it was discovered what she was doing, you would see to it that she was either imprisoned or killed."

"I would never have done that," Creia argued.

"Of course you would have," Ryan said. "You would have

absolutely no problem punishing her in the exact way that you would have punished anyone else who was attempting to do that. And when you did, Earth would have responded. There would have been a military response and it would have been quick and fierce. I would have gotten exactly what I wanted...you presented to me for my own use. I would be rid of Eden, she would have paid for the humiliation that she had put me through, and I would have the chance to continue the work that my family had started. At least, that's what I thought was going to happen. That's what I had planned. I never suspected that she would admit what she was doing. She ruined everything for me. She destroyed the entire plan and made it so that I didn't feel like I had any options anymore. But now I do."

"I won't do anything for you."

"You already have," Ryan told him. "Of course it's not the same as it could have been. You are not here so that I can use you directly, but that doesn't mean that you aren't helping me. Every time that I have attached you to this screen I am also attaching you to the lab itself. I have been feeding your fear and your anger into my system, and that is exactly what I have needed. I will continue to use you until there is nothing left. It will be easy to go from there. It's not like I don't have other Denynso right at my fingertips now. In fact, I have your bloodline so close all I have to do is go after them. It is only a matter of time now before I am able to complete my plan." He paused and gave a low chuckle. "You know, it's a bonus that I get everything I wanted and still get to seek revenge on Eden."

7

———

"A re you alright?"

Ivy stepped into the bedroom of the small Denynso house that she had stayed in for the short time that she had spent on the compound as Maxim turned toward her. He was carefully unpacking everything in his bags and laying the items out on the bed. She knew that he was taking note of what he had and what he might need for the journey that lay ahead of them. The systematic concentration in his movements, however, told her that there was more to the process than just ensuring that they were prepared for the mission that lay ahead of them. He seemed to be distracting himself with the process, letting himself focus all of his energy and effort on going through their supplies rather than the thoughts that were really on his mind.

"Why did he leave?" he asked.

"Creia?" Ivy asked.

"My father."

"What do you mean?" she asked, walking further into the

room so that she could stand beside her partner and run her hand along his back.

"My mother and Athan both said that he was different before he left for that battle. He knew that something was going to happen. Why did he leave?"

Ivy let out a breath.

"I obviously never knew your father, but from what I have learned about him from what I've heard everyone saying about him, he was extremely dedicated to what the Order once was and to doing what was right. He knew something about the Klimnu and the heads of the Order, and it was important to him that he did what he needed to do to resolve it in whatever way that he could. I don't know what that was and I don't know what he had planned to do, but he left because he knew that he had to."

"Did he?"

"Do you?"

Maxim turned to look at her and she saw the familiar softness in his eyes that she had fallen so desperately in love with.

"I won't stop until I feel like I've done everything that I can for my father."

"And he was doing everything that he could for his kind and for you."

Maxim opened his arms to her and Ivy stepped into them, letting him draw her close so that she could feel his heartbeat against her chest.

"What do you think that Creia went after?" he asked.

Ivy stepped back and looked at him, shaking her head.

"I don't know," she admitted. "Theia said that he wanted to know more about the clan that used to live in the other settlement, but that compound was completely destroyed.

You saw it as well as I did. He said that the enemies came in and ensured that it would continue burning forever. What could he possibly find there?"

"There has to be something," Maxim said. "There has to be some reason that he left the compound, especially when most of the warriors aren't here."

"I feel like he did that on purpose."

"Why?"

"He might not have wanted the warriors to know that he was leaving. Maybe he thought that he was only going to be gone for a short time and that he would know what he needed to and be back before everyone returned. That's why he specifically waited until the group had left for Earth before he left."

"What do you think we're going to find out there?" Maxim asked.

"I don't know," Ivy said.

She felt like those were words that she was saying more now that she had in her entire life.

"There's something out there," he said. "Something that I'm afraid will link Creia and what happened to my father. It can't be a coincidence that both of them were drawn to the badlands right before they disappeared."

"Your father didn't die in the badlands, though. He was in battle."

"But my mother said that he had traveled to the badlands because of the Klimnu." He let out a breath and leaned forward to rest a gentle kiss to her lips. "I am going to take a shower before we leave," he said.

Ivy nodded and watched him walk out of the bedroom toward the bathroom. She heard the water running and turned to look at everything that Maxim had spread out across the bed. She wished that there was more that she could do for him. The brief time that she thought that she had lost him had made her feel as though her heart had been torn from her chest and she couldn't bear the thought of feeling like she could let him slip through her fingers again. Thoughts of returning to Earth were completely gone from her mind now and she hated that she had ever let them alienate him. She had been so insistent about not wanting to be on Uoria and wishing that she hadn't come, and now that she had felt what it was to miss Maxim she wished that she had never said them. It hurt her to know that she had ever made him think that she didn't want to be with him or that she wouldn't do everything that it took to stay with him. Now she couldn't even begin to think about leaving Uoria. Maxim was her home and wherever he was, was where she would be.

She listened to the sounds of the water for a few more moments before going into the bathroom. Maxim's clothing was scattered on the floor and she let hers join it. Ivy moved the curtain aside and stepped into the shower behind Maxim. She came up close behind him and wrapped her arms around his waist, leaning forward to rest her head on his back as her hands smoothed up his belly onto his chest. The warmth of his skin comforted her and she relaxed into the feeling of her body molding against his and the hot water washing down over them. Maxim's hand covered hers on his chest and his other came around to hold her hip, pulling her closer.

Ivy kissed his back and nuzzled his skin with her face, stroking his chest with her thumb.

"I love you," she whispered.

"I love you," he whispered back, leaning back so that his head rested on her shoulder.

Ivy pulled her arms from around him and filled her

palm with some of the thick, shimmering body wash that was still left in the shower from when she had first moved into the small home. She held her palm under the water briefly, allowing it to turn the gel into lush bubbles and the steam to carry the sweet smell throughout the space. She carefully spread the bubbles along his skin, washing him tenderly. It was a quiet gesture, one she hoped would show him how deeply she truly loved him and how devoted she was to taking care of him.

Her hands moved along his back and across his shoulders, then down his arms so that she leaned forward and pressed her breasts to his back as she washed his hands. Her fingertips followed the deep dip of his spine between his strong muscles and then along his hips.

Finally he turned and gathered her into his arms, pulling her under the water with him. He held her close, tenderly kissing his way down her neck. She could feel his body responding to her and subtly brushed against him. Maxim's hands ran along the side of her ribs and her waist then slipped around to grip her. Their mouths met and played across each other as Ivy indulged herself by running her hands along his body. The feeling of his muscles rippling beneath her palms was hypnotizing and she felt her craving for him building even more within her.

Maxim led her backwards until she was against the wall and parted their lips. He looked at her with hunger in his eyes and lowered himself to his knees in front of her. His mouth slid down her body, his tongue occasionally touched her skin, bringing shivers of pleasure through her. They settled between her legs and Maxim followed them, drawing his tongue through her core. Ivy's eyes closed and her head fell back against the wall as the feeling jolted through her. Maxim swept one up beneath her leg and lifted it up so that she opened more to him and pressed his mouth closer. She couldn't withhold the sounds pouring from her lips as he continued to nurture her with his tongue and lips. Her hand ran through his hair and settled at the back of his head.

She felt like she was spiraling out of control and she tilted her hips toward his mouth seeking more of the incredible sensations that he was creating within her. She was just on the edge of oblivion when he suddenly rose to his feet, lifting her leg higher and burying his long, thick erection in her in one smooth movement. Ivy cried out at the feeling of him filling her and wrapped her arms around him, pulling him closer. Maxim held her leg around his waist and rolled his hips to drive deeply into her. As he thrust into her, Ivy lifted onto the ball of her supporting foot and then lifted it, wrapping it around him so that both of her legs were around his waist.

Maxim grabbed her by her hips and drove into her harder, using the position to his advantage by stepping slightly away from the wall so that she was at an angle. This allowed him to move harder and faster, pushing so far into her that he created a delirious pleasure that was just on the edge of being overwhelming. He felt impossibly hard within her and her body cradled him like it was crafted specifically for him. It was a feeling so beyond anything that she had ever experienced, something beyond just the physical to a place that was truly transcendent.

Ivy felt Maxim thrust into her one final hard time and roared as he pulsed against her walls. The feeling sent her tumbling over the edge and her own climax responded to his, clutching him so that their bodies melded further and she welcomed his essence into her.

When the waves of their orgasms eased, Ivy lowered her

legs and they slid to the bottom of the shower, allowing the now cool water to wash over them as their bodies tangled and their mouths leisurely explored each other. Ivy rested her head on Maxim's chest and let her fingers trace along Maxim's body, enjoying the contrast between the heat of his skin and the cool of the water. Finally they knew that as much as they wanted to hang on to these precious moments and pretend that there was nothing else for them to be doing, their time was running short and they needed to leave. They climbed out of the shower and dressed slowly, reluctantly, before carefully repacking and leaving to meet the others at the main hall where Theia had gathered further supplies for them.

Ivy WATCHED as each of the members of their group picked up their bags. Emerie had a somewhat frightened look in her eyes but kept her expression steady and strong. Ivy admired her courage. She knew how overwhelming and scary it was to be at the edge of a quest into a completely unknown world that held challenges and threats she couldn't even begin to imagine. Ivy remember how she felt when she realized that her time in the Denynso compound was going to be nothing like she had first imagined and that she would in fact be leaving it to help those on the outside. At least then there was a clear reason for them to leave the compound. They knew what it was that they were doing and why they were doing it. Now they were faced with a totally dark road ahead. They knew only that they needed to find Creia. None of them had ever been in the badlands or knew what was there.

As she looked at her, though, Ivy remembered that

Emerie was not a woman who had just come from Earth and found herself thrust into this type of experience. Instead she was a woman who had left home when she was very young, climbed aboard a spaceship, and left for a planet that she had never seen and that was filled with a cruel and unpredictable species. This was a woman who had found herself crashed and stranded on a planet that she hadn't even known existed until they arrived and had not crumbled. She had spent fifteen years rebuilding her life and then survived an attack that was meant to kill everyone in the settlement. This was a woman who could handle whatever may be waiting for them. Emerie might have fear in her eyes, but she had steel in her blood.

Theia stepped up to Maxim and took his hands between hers.

"Thank you, Maxim. Please, stay safe." She stepped back and took Ivy's hand in one of hers and Athan's in the other. "Stay safe all of you."

Nylek and Mina embraced tightly and Ivy could see Mina's hand gripping the back of his shirt as he held her. She could sense the pain coming off of her and Ivy felt a pang. Nylek was fulfilling his duty to the clan and to his king, but that didn't change how difficult it was for her to watch the man she loved walking away without knowing what he was facing and when, or even if, he would return.

They stepped out of the meeting hall and into the soft sunlight of a gradually deepening afternoon. Athan had told them that it wasn't safe to bring the Mikana vehicles and had hidden them before they gathered their supplies so they took off on foot as they had when Creia led them to the ledge. They walked in silence, their own thoughts fueling them forward. Finally they reached the ledge and climbed to the top, seeming to follow in the same footsteps that they had the first time. Maxim was the first to reach the plateau and Ivy came up to stand beside him. She followed his gaze and looked out over the burning destruction of the badlands.

TBC

(To be continued in book IX...)